MILO'S PET EGG

For Clementine, Toby & Matthew
— my inspirations

Bloomsbury Publishing, London, Berlin and New York

First published in Great Britain in August 2010 by Bloomsbury Publishing Plc
36 Soho Square, London, W1D 3QY

Text & illustrations copyright © Rebecca Elliott 2010
The moral right of the author/illustrator has been asserted

A CIP catalogue record of this book is available from the British Library

ISBN 978 1 4088 0200 7

1 3 5 7 9 10 8 6 4 2

Printed in China by Hung Hing Printing (China) Co Ltd, Shenzhen, Guangdong

All papers used by Bloomsbury Publishing are natural, recyclable products
made from wood grown in well-managed forests. The manufacturing processes
conform to the environmental regulations of the country of origin

www.bloomsbury.com/childrens

MILO'S PET EGG

Rebecca Elliott

BLOOMSBURY

LONDON BERLIN NEW YORK

M ilo was having fun clambering through the trees, when he suddenly noticed something strange in the grass below.

Perhaps it's just a pretty pebble, thought Milo.

He prodded it to be certain.

But to his surprise,
it moved!

Milo carefully put his ear to the pebble.
To his amazement, it was **breathing**.

It was alive!

Milo looked around for the owner of the breathing pebble.

But he could not find anyone.

'Well, it looks like I'll have to take care of you!' declared Milo. 'I'll call you, erm, Snappy.'

From that moment on, Milo and Snappy went everywhere together.

Milo showed Snappy how to swing . . .

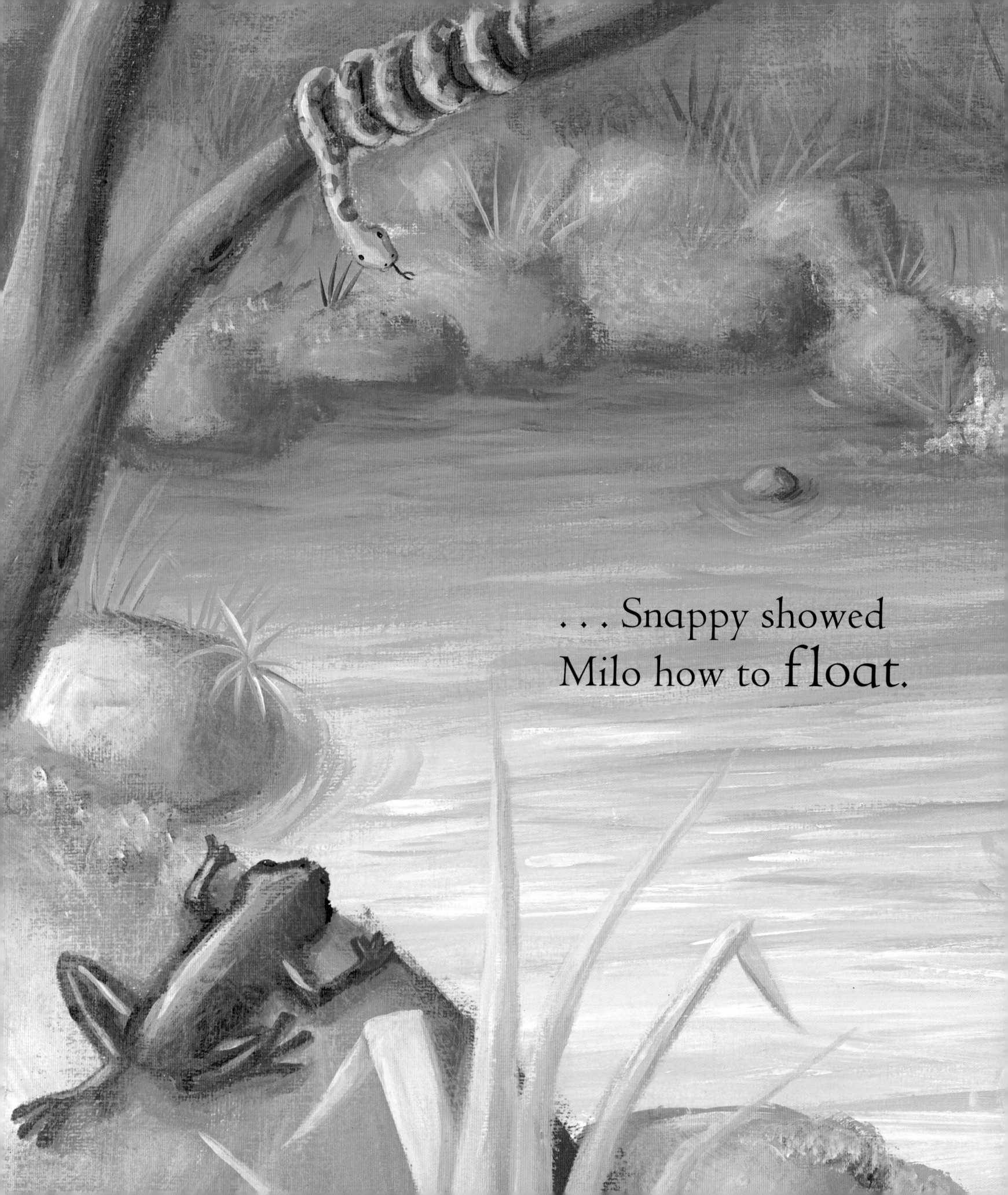

. . . Snappy showed
Milo how to float.

Milo showed Snappy

how to balance . . .

. . . Snappy showed Milo
how to fall.

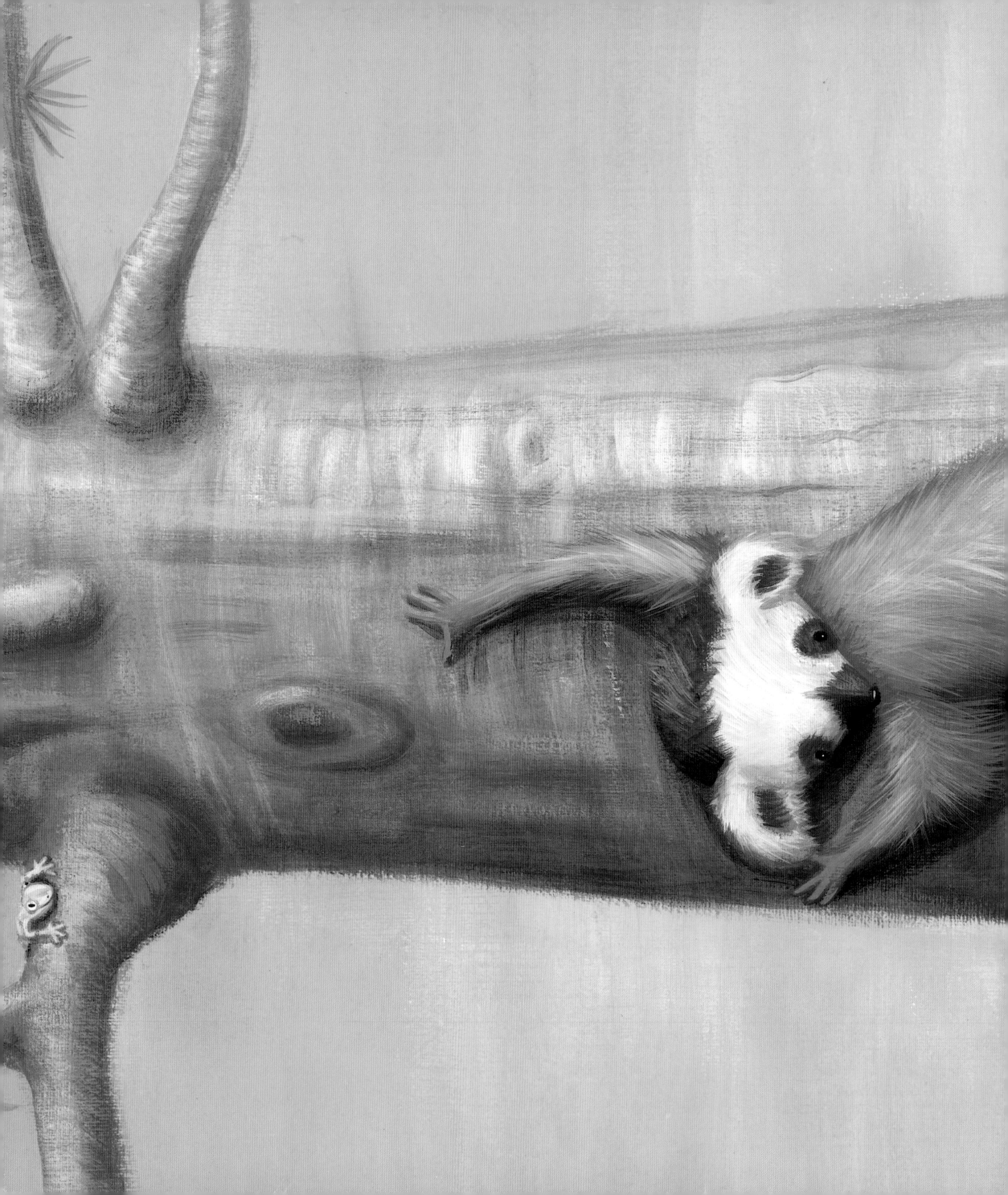

Milo showed Snappy how to climb . . .

. . . Snappy showed Milo how to roll.

All this swinging, floating, balancing, falling, climbing and rolling made them very tired. Now it was time to sleep.

Morning came
and, to Milo's horror,
Snappy was in pieces.
'Oh no! Snappy is
broken,' he wailed.

'Hang on a minute. Who
are you? Where did
you come from?'
asked Milo.

Milo soon realised who it was.

'Snappy!' he exclaimed with delight.
'**Now** I know who you belong to!
Come on, I'll take you home.'

'Excuse me, madam,' said Milo, 'but I think you might have lost something.'

'My baby!' cried Mrs Croc. She turned to Milo. 'Is there anything I can do to thank you?'

'Just one thing,' answered Milo. 'If you ever need a crocodile-sitter, I'd be happy to help out.'

'I'd like that,' said Mrs Croc.

'So would I,' squeaked Snappy.